To Madelynn,

Enjoy!

Andrew Toffoli

hi·stories®

GEORGE WASHINGTON

Based on the life of the first president of the United States, George Washington

Written and Illustrated by:
ANDREW TOFFOLI

Color Design by:
MARIA GONZALEZ

GEORGE WASHINGTON

Printed in China

ISBN 978-0-9763233-6-5

Library of Congress Control Number: 2009925909

Our mission is to educate children about history while using humor and imagination to teach valuable life lessons.

Please visit us online at: **www.littlegerm.com**

10 9 8 7 6 5 4 3 2 1

For Stella

George WashingTON,
a persistent pachyderm,
was born in
Pope's Creek, Virginia in 1732.

While living in Virginia,
which was one of the thirteen colonies,
George loved to ride horses and play game
on his farm.

His favorite game was follow the leader...
and George was always the leader.

In school, George was a math virtuoso,
but his spelling skills were a little so-so.

George loved numbers so much he became a surveyor. This is someone who measures forests and fields.

Surveys were very important, because they showed every farmer where his fence should go.

When all of the farms were measured,
George volunteered to guard
the land the king treasured.

All of the land was ruled by an English king
who lived far across the sea,
and who liked to drink lots and lots of tea.

One day the king was reviewing the bills for all of the land he owned.

He noticed how
his stack of bills got
higher...

and higher...

and higher...

...until they were as tall as a church spire!

The bills were more than the king could afford.

The king had to make more
money to pay the bills.

He figured it out
and shouted
"I will tax everything
including my tea
and collect lots and
lots of money!"

The new taxes made the colonists shout,
"No taxation without representation!"
They wanted a say in this situation.

So, late one night at Boston Harbor,
the townspeople created a commotion.

Dressed as Indians, they dumped all of the
king's precious tea into the ocean.
TEA
TEA

This night would go down in history as the Boston Tea Party.
It made the king very, very angry!

So, the king sent his soldiers to make the colonists pay, and they said "No Way!"

This made the king furious and he declared war on the thirteen colonies.

Hearing of this news,
the townspeople met under
the Liberty Tree
to elect a leader secretly.

The people formed the Colonial Army
and chose George as their leader.

The revolution
lasted eight years...

...and each side fought
through temperatures
from over 100 to below zero.

With George WashingTON's wits and determination, the colonists won the war and George became a national hero.

The thirteen colonies became the thirteen states and everyone was feeling great!

All ties to England were torn
and the United States was born.

An election would give
the people a voice,
and the president would be
the man of their choice.

The people elected
George WashingTon
as the first president
and it was a huge event.

George WashingTON was
born to lead.
He was a general, the first
president of the United States
and the father of our country.

Words to know:

ommotion: Noun- a noisy confusion.

ommunity: Noun- a group of people who live close together or who have the same interests.

lection: Noun- the process of choosing a person to serve in government by voting.

achyderm: Noun- any of several very thick-skinned, hoofed mammals such as the elephant, ippopotamus, and rhinoceros.

ersistent: Adjective- holding on in a firm, steady way.

evolution: Noun- the act of removing a government by force and putting a new government n its place.

pire: Noun- a tall, narrow, upward structure shaped like a cone on the outside of a building.

irtuoso: Noun- a person who demonstrates exceptional ability, style, or skill.

Vit: Noun- the ability to understand, think, or know.

George Washington Carfur™
Coming Soon from
hi·stories®
Marco Hippolo™
Abrahound Lincoln™
Ludpig Van Beethoven™

JoHorn Gutenberg™
Susan Bee Anthony™
Juan Ponce De LeBison™
Bark Twain™
Sir Ibis Newton™
Namolean Bonaparte™